Dear Parent:
Your child's love of reading starts here!

Every child learns to read in a different way and at his or her own speed. Some go back and forth between reading levels and read favorite books again and again. Others read through each level in order. You can help your young reader improve and become more confident by encouraging his or her own interests and abilities. From books your child reads with you to the first books he or she reads alone, there are I Can Read Books for every stage of reading:

SHARED READING
Basic language, word repetition, and whimsical illustrations, ideal for sharing with your emergent reader

BEGINNING READING
Short sentences, familiar words, and simple concepts for children eager to read on their own

READING WITH HELP
Engaging stories, longer sentences, and language play for developing readers

READING ALONE
Complex plots, challenging vocabulary, and high-interest topics for the independent reader

I Can Read Books have introduced children to the joy of reading since 1957. Featuring award-winning authors and illustrators and a fabulous cast of beloved characters, I Can Read Books set the standard for beginning readers.

A lifetime of discovery begins with the magical words "I Can Read!"

Visit www.icanread.com for information
on enriching your child's reading experience.

The Berenstain Bears: We Love Our Teacher!
Copyright © 2024 by Berenstain Publishing, Inc.
All rights reserved. Printed in the United States of America.
No part of this book may be used or reproduced in any manner whatsoever without written permission except in the case of brief quotations embodied in critical articles and reviews. For information address HarperCollins Children's Books, a division of HarperCollins Publishers, 195 Broadway, New York, NY 10007.
www.icanread.com

Library of Congress Control Number: 2023943266
ISBN 978-0-06-335537-8 (trade bdg.) — ISBN 978-0-06-335536-1 (pbk.)

Design by Jon Corby
24 25 26 27 28 LB   10 9 8 7 6 5 4 3 2 1
First Edition

The Berenstain Bears

WE L♥VE OUR TEACHER!

Mike Berenstain

Based on the characters created by
Stan and Jan Berenstain

HARPER
An Imprint of HarperCollinsPublishers

Brother and Sister like school.
Last year, they really liked
their teachers.
But this is the start of
a new school year.
Who will their new teachers be?

Brother's new teacher
is Miz Bearly.

"Uh-oh!" Brother says.

She looks a little grumpy.

She seems a little grouchy.

Will Brother like

his new teacher?

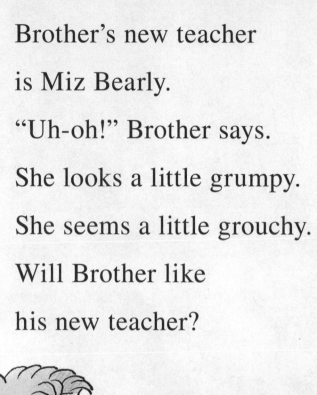

Miz Bearly calls the cubs' names.

"Brother Bear!" she calls.

"Here!" says Brother.

"Brother?" says Miz Bearly.

"What kind of name is that?

Don't you have a name

like Bill or Joe?"

"No," says Brother. "Just Brother."

"Hmm!" says Miz Bearly.

Miz Bearly is a tough teacher.

She gives out lots of homework.

She gives lots of tests.

But she is a good teacher.

Miz Bearly knows a lot.

She knows about history and science.

She knows about things like dinosaurs and outer space.

Miz Bearly makes learning fun!

Miz Bearly teaches her class about the moon and planets. She has the class come to school after dark.

Other students and their families
can come, too.

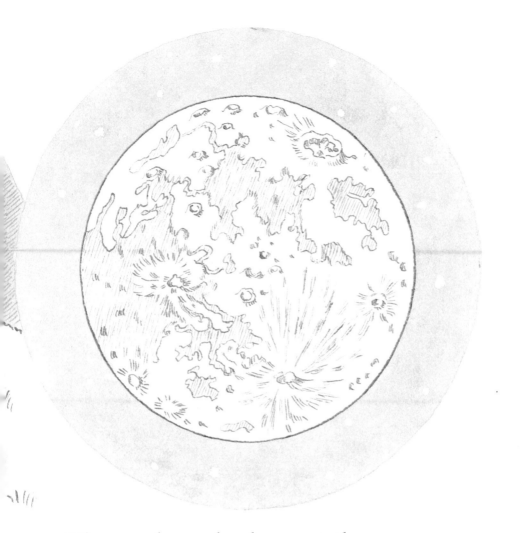

The students look up at the moon.

It looks very big!

You can see big holes

and rocks on the moon.

The cubs have lots of fun!

17

Miz Bearly teaches her class
about the past.
They take a school trip
to see an old water mill.

Other classes and families
come, too.
The cubs see how things were
made long ago.

The class sees big wheels turning.

Brother cranks a crank.

Sister pulls a rope.

The cubs learn about tools.

All the bears have lots of fun!

Miz Bearly teaches her class
how things are made in today's world.
She brings in a friend who worked
on planes for the Bear Air Force.

Her friend shows the class

the tools she used to make planes.

They are really noisy!

But everyone has lots of fun!

The school year goes by fast.

It is time for a break.

The cubs will be back soon.

They will miss Miz Bearly.

The class thinks Miz Bearly

is a good teacher.

They want her to know that,
so they make her a big card.

Millie
Brother
Ted
Emma
WE
OUR
Barry
Nora
Bonnie
Harry
Queenie
Linda

Can it be?

There is a tear in Miz Bearly's eye.

She is a big softy!

Goodbye, Miz Bearly!

See you soon!